Aio the Rainmaker

FIONA FRENCH

London   OXFORD UNIVERSITY PRESS   1975

The people of the village gathered
together at the end of the dry season.
After they had planted the new crops they
danced and sang in honour of their Ancestors.

And they sang the story of Aio the Rainmaker:
How he visited the Ancestors,
And how they sent rain to their children.

'Many years ago', they sang, 'the rain did not fall at the end
of the dry season, so the new crops died,
and the rivers turned into dust.
The people were so thirsty, they begged Aio
the Rainmaker to make the rain:
  "We have nothing to drink, Aio.
  We have nothing to eat,
  All our crops are dead,
  Send us the rain, Aio."

"All the animals are dying.
The leopard and antelope lie all day in the shade of the
baobab tree.
All the animals in the forest are still and silent,
Even the python and the scorpion are thirsty.
Go up to the high rocks and speak to the Ancestors, Aio.
Ask them to send us the rain, Aio,
Send us the rain, or we shall die."

'Aio the Rainmaker went up to the high rocks.
He called to the Ancestors in their dark kingdom,
He danced to the rhythm of the far-off drums,
He told the Ancestors that the people would die
if there was no rain:
    "All our crops are dead,
    All the animals are dying."

'Aio danced and imitated the leopard.
"I am the leopard, the cunning leopard,
but I am so thirsty, I have no strength to
chase the antelope. All I can do is lie all day
in the shade of the baobab tree."

'Aio danced as if he were the antelope.
    "I am the antelope, who leaps and runs from the
    cunning leopard. But now I have lost my strength.
    I am so thirsty I lie all day
    in the shade of the baobab tree.

"All the animals on the grassland are still,
All the animals in the forest are silent.
I am the chameleon, but I have no strength
to change my colour."
'Aio danced as if he were the chameleon.

nd he danced as if he were the parrot:
    "I am the parrot who cannot fly,
    I am so thirsty.

"The monkeys in the trees
sit in silence all day long.
Even the frogs sing no more in the evening.

"Even the rock python is so thirsty she
has no strength to shed her skin.
Even the scorpion cannot carry her children.
Ancestors, what is left for us,
when even the python cannot leave its old skin?"

'Aio's song was so sorrowful that the Ancestors
came out of their dark kingdom. They crowded the sky and
made it dark and stormy.
    "Aio, we hear your song,
    And we will send rain to our children.
    What will they give us in return?
    What will our children give us?"

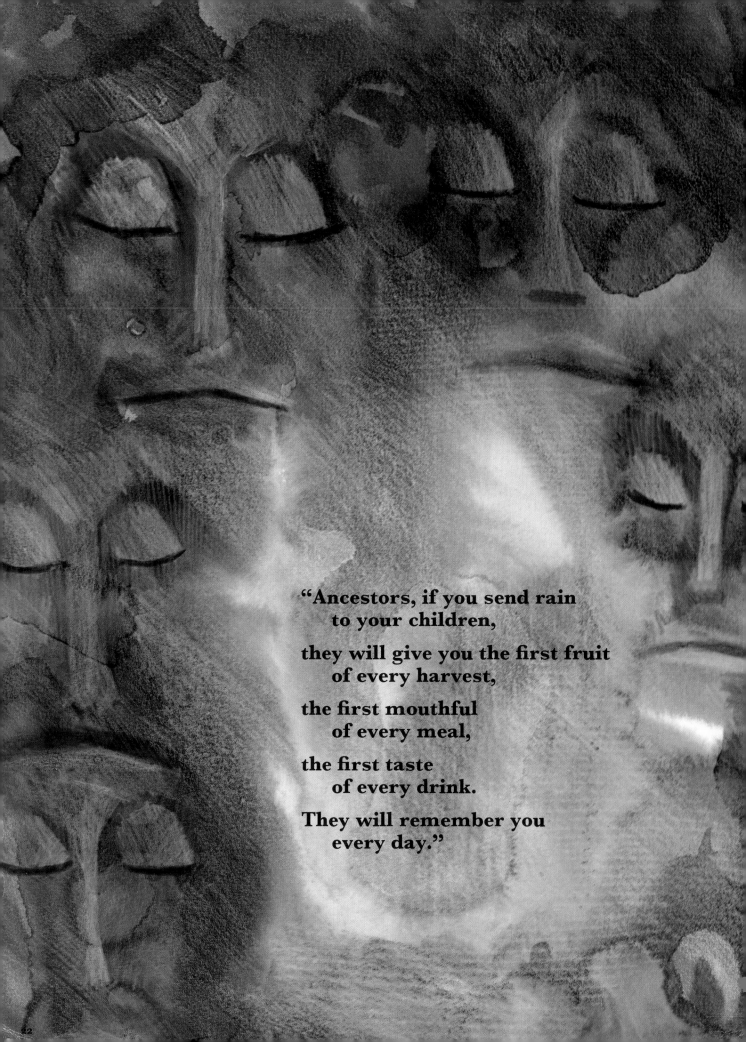

"Ancestors, if you send rain
    to your children,

they will give you the first fruit
    of every harvest,

the first mouthful
    of every meal,

the first taste
    of every drink.

They will remember you
    every day."

"If you remember us, Aio,
and your children remember us,
and your children's children,
then we shall send you rain.
But if you should ever forget,
we will keep it in our kingdom,
and your crops will die."

'So the rain fell. First it came as a shower, that fell gently on the plains, making them green again.

'But as Aio went back through the forest
the rain fell in a torrent, like a waterfall,
and rivulets filled all the cracks in the ground.
The forest was green, the leaves shone darkly,
and the orchids showed all their bright colours.'

And the people of the village
listened to the words of Aio the Rainmaker, and always afterwards
they remembered the Ancestors at the end of the dry season.
That is why they dance and sing, and tell the story

Of Aio the Rainmaker.
How he visited the Ancestors,
And how they sent the rain to their children
Many years ago.

Oxford University Press, Ely House, London W1 Glasgow New York Toronto Melbourne Wellington Cape Town Ibadan Nairobi Dar Es Salaam Lusaka Addis Ababa Delhi Bombay Calcutta Madras Karachi Lahore Dacca Kuala Lumpur Singapore Hong Kong Tokyo ISBN 0 19 279704 2 © Fiona French 1975 First Published 1975 Printed in Holland *All rights reserved. No part of this publication may be reproduced, stored in a retrieval system, or transmitted, in any form or by any means, electronic, mechanical, photocopying, recording or otherwise, without the prior permission of Oxford University Press*